Todd's TV

James Proimos

 KATHERINE TEGEN BOOKS
An Imprint of HarperCollins Publishers

Katherine Tegen Books is an imprint of HarperCollins Publishers.

Todd's TV
Copyright © 2010 by James Proimos
All rights reserved. Manufactured in China.
No part of this book may be used or reproduced in any manner whatsoever without
written permission except in the case of brief quotations embodied in critical articles
and reviews. For information address HarperCollins Children's Books, a division of
HarperCollins Publishers, 10 East 53rd Street, New York, NY 10022.
www.harpercollinschildrens.com

Library of Congress Cataloging-in-Publication Data
Proimos, James.
Todd's TV / words and pictures by James Proimos. — 1st ed.
p. cm.
Summary: When Todd's parents are too busy to take care of him,
his television steps in to handle the parenting.
ISBN 978-0-06-170985-2 (trade bdg.)   ISBN 978-0-06-170987-6 (lib. bdg.)
[1. Television—Fiction. 2. Parents—Fiction.] I. Title.
PZ7.P9432To 2010   [E]—dc22   2009018507   CIP   AC

Typography by Rachel Zegar
10 11 12 13 14 LEO 10 9 8 7 6 5 4 3 2 1
❖
First Edition

For Brenda Bowen

This is Todd's mom.

This is Todd.

This is Todd's dad.

And this is Todd's TV.

Todd loved his parents.

But he had grown much closer to his TV.

It made sense.

Whenever the phone rang, Todd was told to go watch TV.

Whenever it rained outside, Todd's parents put him in front of the TV.

Whenever they had "parent things" to discuss,
Todd's mom and dad pointed him to the TV.
This is just how things are.
Parents are busy people.
They can't spend every minute with their child.

One night Todd's parents were trying
to decide which of them could take
Todd to his parent-teacher conference.

Todd and his parents rushed into the other room to see who the voice belonged to.

They were surprised when it turned out to be the TV.

"The TV is right," said Todd's mom.

 "The TV has always been good at watching our boy," said Todd's dad.

So off the TV and Todd went to the parent-teacher conference.

When they got to school, all the other
parents gave the TV a strange look.

But the TV was very entertaining.
Soon all the parents were talking
about how great the TV was.

The teacher said Todd had been acting
out a lot lately. The TV assured her
that things would change.

Afterward, the TV took Todd out for ice cream.

That night, while Todd's dad was still at work, the TV tucked Todd in.

The next morning Todd's mom was exhausted from her meeting, so the TV made the pancakes.

Soon the TV was driving
Todd to school each day.

Giving heart-to-heart advice.

Playing catch.

Todd's parents were grateful the TV
was able to take Todd on vacations
when they were unavailable.

They were happy when the TV showed
Todd things he had never seen before.

They began to miss Todd, although they did
see him at dinner, where the TV would perform
stand-up comedy while they ate together.

Then one night the TV said something to Todd that threw his parents for a loop.

Todd's parents were outraged.

Todd's dad had several meetings with the TV. But the TV would always change the subject and wind up talking him into buying products he didn't really need.

TV, YOU ARE GOING TO HAVE TO BACK OFF.

IF YOU ACT NOW, I CAN GET YOU A FULL SET OF CUTLERY FOR THE LOW, LOW PRICE OF $9.99! BUT THAT'S NOT ALL!

Todd's mom tried outperforming the TV on several occasions. But the TV was far more talented than her.

They even tried dressing up as a TV themselves.

But nothing seemed to work.

Todd loved all the attention. But he missed his parents as much as they missed him. So he did something he hoped would give his parents an idea.

And it did.

Todd's parents ran over to the TV and did something they should have done a long time ago.

They turned the TV off.

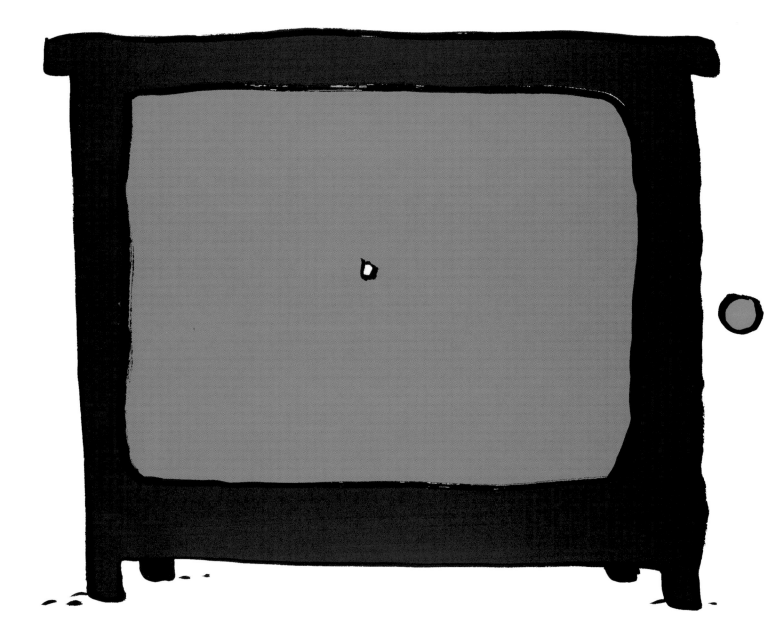

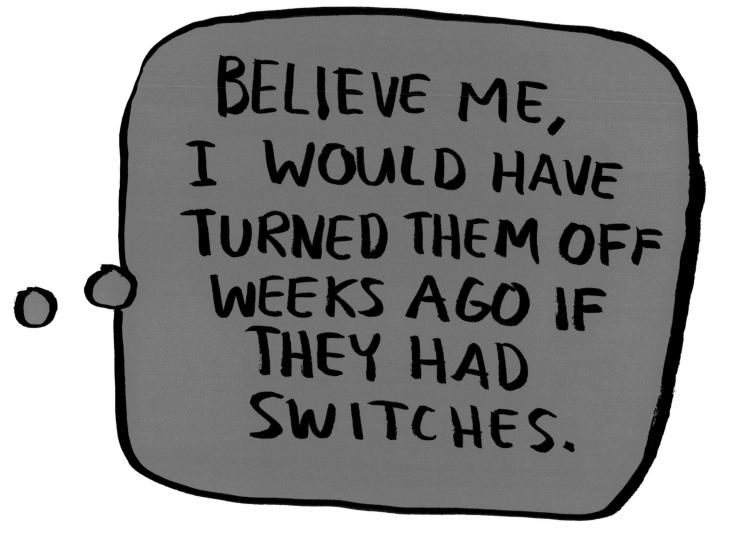

From that point on, Todd and his parents spent huge amounts of quality time together.

Todd read more.

Listened better.

And felt more loved than he ever had in his life.

Things went on like that for a full year. No one was surprised when Todd won the Student of the Year Award.

First prize: a super-duper high-tech computer with all the bells and whistles.